RR JC

JUL 2023

THE GOLEM'S GAME!

© 2023 Mojang AB. All Rights Reserved. Minecraft, the Minecraft logo, the Mojang Studios logo and the Creeper logo are trademarks of the Microsoft group of companies.

Published in the United States by Random House Children's Books, a division of Penguin Random House LLC, 1745 Broadway, New York, NY 10019, and in Canada by Penguin Random House Canada Limited, Toronto. Random House and the colophon are registered trademarks of Penguin Random House LLC.

rhcbooks.com
minecraft.net

Library of Congress Cataloging-in-Publication Data is available upon request.
ISBN 978-0-593-56291-8 (trade) — ISBN 978-0-593-56292-5 (lib. bdg.) —
ISBN 978-0-593-56293-2 (ebook)

Cover design by Diane Choi

Printed in the United States of America
1st Printing

THE GOLEM'S GAME!

By Nick Eliopulos
Illustrated by Alan Batson and Chris Hill

Random House 🏠 New York

MORGAN

ASH

HARPER

PLAYERS!

PO

JODI

THEO

PROLOGUE

Morgan Mercado was alone in the Nether.

Usually, Morgan explored Minecraft with a whole team—his friends. Usually, a few hostile mobs would not be any reason to worry. Usually.

But today Morgan did not have his team with him. And there were more than a few mobs to worry about.

Morgan crept low, hoping that he wouldn't be spotted. The dark, crumbling castle he was in offered many places to hide. But the castle was crawling with piglins. They were piglike mobs, and they did not take kindly to trespassers.

Morgan couldn't turn back, though. There was something of immense value in this fortress. And going back to his friends empty-handed simply wasn't an option.

A bloodcurdling squeal rang through the air. Morgan knew he'd been spotted.

Sneaking was no longer an option, either. Fortunately, he had the best sword and armor in the game. He was more than a match for a piglin or two. Or three. Maybe four . . .

But the piglins kept coming! There were more of them than he could count.

Morgan leapt into battle. With his sword in front of him, he carved a path through an endless wave of enemies.

One after another, the piglins fell to Morgan's blade. But it seemed like for every one that went down, two took its place. And even through his armor, Morgan could feel their attacks.

He knew it was only a matter of time before . . . **well, best not to think about it and just keep swinging.**

Chapter 1

MORGAN MERCADO: STAR OF TRACK AND FIELD! OR MAYBE HE'S MORE LIKE A METEOR, CRASHING AND BURNING SPECTACULARLY!

Woodsword Middle School had been **transformed overnight.** Colorful pennants hung from the low ceilings, and the hallways were decorated with posters that offered words of encouragement to the students.

One poster showed a cartoon brain with arms, legs, and sunglasses lifting weights. A banner above it said: WINNER!

Another poster said: WINNERS NEVER QUIT! It featured a group of smiling kids all holding up gleaming medals.

And a third: TEAMWORK MAKES THE DREAM WORK! It showed a squirrel, a chipmunk, and a

WINNER!

hamster standing atop one another's shoulders in order to reach a steaming pie on a high window ledge.

Jodi Mercado smiled. She loved color and art, and above all else, she loved animals. **However, she was pretty sure that hamsters didn't eat pie.** (She decided to test that theory as soon as possible with the class hamster, Baron Sweetcheeks, and the library's official mascot, Duchess Dimples.)

"Hey, Jodi!" a familiar voice called out. She turned to see her friend **Po Chen.** He sounded full of energy, as usual. "Do you like what we've done with the place?"

"I love it," said Jodi, nodding enthusiastically. "But why are you decorating?"

"This Friday is Field Day," said Shelly Silver. She was in student government with Po. Once they had been challengers for class president, but now they worked side by side. "We're going to be celebrating all week."

"Field Day!" said Jodi, slapping her own forehead. "I almost forgot. My brother isn't going to be happy about this."

"Why not?" said Po. "He's on a team with Harper and Theo, isn't he?"

"There might be a small complication," said Jodi. "I had better find **Harper** and **Theo.**

Keep up the good work!"

Jodi gave Po and Shelly each a thumbs-up (two thumbs total), then she ducked beneath the hanging pennants and began her search.

She looked for Harper and Theo in the science lab, where they sometimes helped out before school. They weren't there, but Jodi did find their science teacher, Doc Culpepper. The teacher was jumping in place and waving her arms as if trying to get someone's attention. Glass beakers and test tubes rattled with every jump.

"Doc Culpepper?" said Jodi. "What are you doing?"

"Jumping jacks!" answered the teacher. "I'm the coach of Team Red for Field Day, and I've got to be ready!"

Jodi was pretty sure the Field Day coaches only needed to take attendance and hand out ribbons. It was unclear to her what jumping jacks had to do with that. But since Doc seemed laser-focused on her exercise, Jodi just shrugged, gave Doc a little wave, and backed out of the room.

Next, she looked for Harper and Theo in the school's butterfly sanctuary. (It *used* to be a computer lab, but . . . long story.) Her friends weren't there, either, but Ms. Minerva was. Their homeroom teacher sat cross-legged on the floor. Her eyes were closed, and butterflies were resting in her frizzy hair and on her arms and shoulders. One was even perched on her ever-present coffee cup.

"**Ms. Minerva?**" said Jodi. "Are you okay?"

Ms. Minerva jumped with surprise, and the startled butterflies took to the air. "Oh! Jodi, you scared me," said the teacher. "I was meditating. I'm the coach of Team Blue, you see, and I've got to get *in the zone,* as they say."

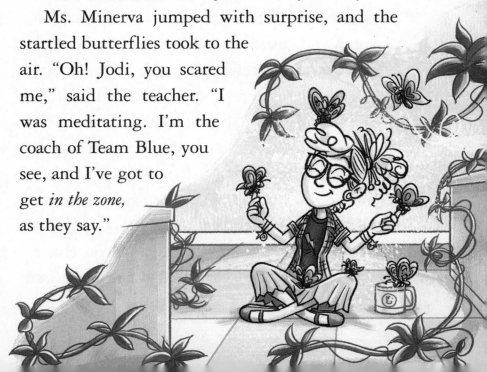

Jodi wasn't sure anybody actually said "in the zone," and she didn't know what meditating had to do with Field Day. But she smiled politely and nodded, and she was careful to close the door gently on her way out.

She finally found her friends outside. They were beneath the large tree in front of the school.

Harper Houston gave Jodi a welcoming hug. "Good morning!" she said. "Theo was just showing me his new shoes."

Theo Grayson lifted one foot. His shoe was clean and bright. "It's designed specifically for running," he said. "It could increase my speed by as much as twelve percent!"

"I'm using my normal shoes," said Harper. "But I learned some new stretches over the weekend. They'll help me run faster, and I won't get as sore."

"What about Morgan?" asked Theo. "Did he practice this weekend? A relay team is only as fast as its slowest member."

"That's what I wanted to talk to you about," said Jodi. She knew that Harper and Theo were

counting on her brother, **Morgan.** The three of them had signed up to be in a relay race for Team Blue. That meant they all had to take turns running as fast as they could.

But there was one problem with that plan.

"Hi, guys," said a voice. "Sorry I'm late."

Jodi recognized her brother's voice immediately. She also recognized the looks on her friends' faces.

Harper immediately looked surprised.

Theo instantly looked worried.

And Morgan already looked frustrated as he limped up to them. He was unsteady on a pair of crutches. His foot was in a brace.

"Morgan, your foot!" said Harper.

"What happened?" asked Theo.

"I had a small accident," said Morgan. "Don't worry, though. **It's just a sprain.** It's not as bad as it looks."

But Jodi did worry. As she watched her brother struggle to balance on his crutches, she worried he would fall over.

"Our pediatrician told you to take it easy," said Jodi. "I thought you'd stay home this week."

"And miss Field Day?" said Morgan. **"No way."**

"Hold on," said Theo. "You still want to be in the race?"

"Morgan, I'm not sure that's a great idea," said Harper.

"It'll be fine," said Morgan. "You'll see."

Then he almost fell, and Jodi caught him.

It was going to be a long week. She could tell.

Chapter 2

BLUE FIRE! GREAT FOR SETTING A SPOOKY SCENE. NOT SO GREAT FOR MAKING S'MORES!

Morgan set one blocky foot in front of the other. **In Minecraft, his injury didn't bother him at all.** It was a relief that he didn't have to worry about it while he was here, inside a hyper-realistic, VR-augmented version of his favorite game.

Of course, there were other things to worry about here.

Morgan and his friends were on a quest to save the Evoker King, a former enemy turned friend. The Evoker King was an artificial intelligence—a digital life-form—who had been split into pieces. So far, they had retrieved four of the pieces. Each time, a digital butterfly had led them where they needed to go. **The butterflies had been an obvious clue,** because they didn't exist in a normal game of Minecraft. And Morgan would know. He prided himself on being an expert on all things Minecraft.

Now, a few butterflies flittered around a rectangular four-by-five-block structure of darkest obsidian. It was a portal to another Minecraft dimension. It glowed purple, daring them to step inside. Morgan's friends were ready to accept that dare. But Morgan wasn't so sure.

"CHECK YOUR INVENTORIES," he said. "Let's make sure we have everything we'll need."

"That sounds impossible," said Harper. "How can we know what we'll need before we need it?"

"We can handle anything the Nether throws at us," said Po. His avatar was wearing a toga, with a laurel circling his head. "We got this far, right?"

"And time is running out," Theo added. "THE FAULT HAS EATEN THE ENTIRE SKY." He pointed to where the Overworld sky had been replaced with a mass of dark, swirling pixels. Every few moments, lightning flashed.

"Morgan, what's wrong?" asked Jodi. "Usually you're the first one to leap into danger."

"In the Overworld, maybe," said Morgan. "BUT THE NETHER IS DIFFERENT."

"We've been there before," said his sister. "Back

when we thought the Evoker King was our enemy, remember?"

Morgan shook his head. "There was an update. The Nether has *changed* since then. **IT'S MORE DANGEROUS THAN EVER.**"

"Well, lucky us!" said Jodi, and she put her blocky hand on Morgan's shoulder. "We have a Minecraft *expert* leading the way."

Morgan grinned, but his heart sank a little. **He had read all about the Nether, of course.** And he had visited on several occasions.

But between the recent school election, and the bee crisis, and Jodi's pet-walking misadventure, he'd been awfully busy. He hadn't traveled to the Nether in quite some time.

And despite how he liked to think of himself as an expert, he had never really mastered all the challenges in the Nether. He realized that might be a problem, but at the moment he didn't think making that particular confession was going to help them. He cleared his throat.

"Let's just keep our eyes open," Morgan said. "I have a feeling . . . **THIS QUEST IS ABOUT TO GET A LOT MORE DANGEROUS.**"

"We can handle it," promised Po.

"Together," added Harper.

"Probably," said Theo.

Morgan nodded, but he was wrestling with his own thoughts. The Fault above them crackled with lightning, and a strange wind seemed to pick up, causing the pixelated grass and leaves to sway. *There is no wind in Minecraft,* he thought. The Fault—**the hole in the game's code that appeared when the Evoker King had**

been broken—was wreaking havoc, causing Minecraft to change in unexpected ways.

Morgan always loved Minecraft. When Doc Culpepper had created a set of VR goggles—goggles that allowed them to travel into the game—his love had only grown. This version of Minecraft was just for them, and it had been a little strange from the start. Morgan didn't know what he would do if they lost it all to the Fault.

"ALL RIGHT," he said. **"BUT WE STICK TOGETHER IN THERE.** And we don't leave anybody behind, no matter what."

Morgan held his breath as he stepped through the portal. He was ready for a fight. But everything was peaceful on the other side of the portal. They were in a clearing within a strange blue-green forest, with tall trees and a thick covering of vines. Someone had set up a campsite, with a series of treasure chests ringing a campfire. The fire burned an eerie shade of blue, and an iron golem stood motionless nearby.

"It looks like a camp," said Jodi. **"IS THAT GOLEM HERE TO GUARD IT?"**

"Let's not loot any treasure chests until we know for sure," said Harper.

"Aw," said Po, who had started reaching for the nearest chest.

"I've never seen a golem that color before," said Theo.

Morgan took a closer look. At first, it was hard to tell. **The Nether was dark, and the blue fire made everything seem a little strange.** Morgan realized that Theo was right about the golem. Morgan had thought it was an iron golem, but they were light gray in color, like iron armor. This one was darker.

"Is that . . . netherite?" he asked.

To his surprise, he got an answer!

"Yes," said the golem, and it turned to gaze at them. **"IT'S ABOUT TIME YOU GOT HERE.** I've been waiting for you. **AND TIME IS OF THE ESSENCE."**

Chapter 3

THE GOLEM SPEAKS! WILL HE TALK ABOUT THE WEATHER, OR ISSUE A DIRE CHALLENGE THAT WILL TEST THE VERY LIMITS OF FRIENDSHIP AND SKILL?

When the golem spoke, Morgan reacted without thinking.

He already had his sword in his hand. And he was on edge, expecting trouble as soon as they'd entered the Nether. The golem seemed like trouble. So when it surprised him by speaking, he lashed out with his sword.

It was a diamond sword. One of the most powerful weapons in Minecraft.

It didn't seem to hurt the golem at all.

"NOW. NOW. THERE'S NO REASON TO BE IMPOLITE," said the golem.

"Uh . . . sorry?" said Morgan. He eyed his sword,

a little awed and irritated that it had had no effect.

"Put that sword away, Morgan!" said Jodi. "You're lucky you didn't cut that poor golem in half!"

"NETHERITE IS MUCH STRONGER THAN DIAMOND," Harper explained. "It's also extremely rare. I've never seen a golem made of it before."

"That's because it isn't possible," said Theo. "Not in a normal game of Minecraft, at least."

Po turned to the golem, his eyes wide with awe. **"YOU'RE WHO WE'RE LOOKING FOR. YOU'RE**

ONE OF THE EVOKER SPAWN."

Morgan thought Po must be correct. When the Evoker King had shattered, he had taken the form of six different mobs. So far, all of the mobs were familiar Minecraft creatures, but with strange powers and personalities. This golem certainly seemed to fit the pattern.

"THAT'S CORRECT," the golem said, its voice rumbling in its massive chest. "When the Evoker King fell, my siblings and I rose in his

place. And you are—"

"We're hoping to put him back together," said Theo, interupting enthusiastically.

"By bringing you and your 'siblings' together," Harper added.

"LIKE A FAMILY REUNION!" Jodi suggested enthusiastically.

"I know what you're doing," said the golem. "Or should I say: I know what you're *trying* to do. But will you succeed? I am not so certain."

"Then help us," said Jodi.

"Yeah!" said Po. **"THAT WOULD BE A NICE CHANGE OF PACE, ACTUALLY."**

The golem swept its bright red eyes over them. It seemed to gaze at

Morgan an especially long time.

"**I WILL GIVE YOU WHAT YOU SEEK,**" said the golem. "I will rejoin with my siblings."

"All right!" said Po.

"But *first* . . . ," continued the golem. "You must pass my test."

Po shrieked in horror, and the golem tilted its head in confusion. "What is wrong with that one?"

"Ignore him," said Jodi. "**HE'S JUST BEING DRAMATIC.**"

"He does hate tests," said Harper.

"**I'M NOT AFRAID OF ANY TEST,**" said Morgan. He squared his shoulders and lifted his chin. The golem still towered above them, but Morgan was determined to show no fear. "You want to test us? Well, so did that witch. And the swarming hive mind."

"Don't forget the creepy cave spider," said Jodi, shuddering.

"And the Endermonster!" said Theo.

"Wow, it really has been a weird few weeks," said Po, scratching his square chin with his block hand.

"My point is, we're undefeated," Morgan told the golem. **"WE'VE PASSED EVERY TEST. WE'VE MASTERED EVERY CHALLENGE.** And we'll survive anything *you* decide to throw at us."

The golem had no mouth. That made it especially strange when it tilted its head back . . . and laughed.

Morgan frowned. "What's so funny?" he demanded.

"You are correct," said the golem. **"SO FAR, YOU HAVE PASSED EVERY TEST . . . AS A TEAM."** Its eyes glittered in the blue campfire. "You have learned to work together. But this time, you will be tested . . . as individuals."

With that, the golem raised its massive slate-gray arm.

"Tomorrow, I will expect one of you to run my

GAUNTLET. ALONE."

It waved its blocklike fist before them, and Morgan's vision filled with purple. He closed his eyes. And when he opened them . . .

He was back in the real world. Back in the Stonesword Library's computer area, with Doc's special VR goggles on his face.

He looked around. His friends were taking off their own goggles. They all looked as surprised as he felt.

"What just happened?" he asked.

Harper shook her head. "It shouldn't be possible. But somehow—"

Theo finished her thought. **"Somehow the Netherite Golem kicked us out of the Minecraft!"**

Chapter 4

P.E.: IT STANDS FOR PIGLIN EDUCATION! HONEST, GO LOOK IT UP. I'LL WAIT.

Morgan needed answers, and Theo was his best chance to get them.

"What just happened, Theo?" he asked. **"And how do we stop it from happening again?"**

"I—I don't know," Theo stammered.

"But you're the team programmer," said Morgan. "You understand computers better than any of us."

"I still have a lot to learn," said Theo. He waved his headset around. "These are the highest of high tech. Even Doc doesn't understand how they work, and she created them!"

"It's all right that you don't have answers,

Theo," said Harper. She placed a steadying hand on his shoulder. "But if you have any *theories,* now is the time to share them."

Theo ran his fingers through his hair. "Well, as you all know, I've been keeping an eye on the game's code. **Ever since the Evoker King transformed, there's been a hole in that code."**

"Right," said Po. "That's why we're trying to put the guy back together again. **We're hoping that will fix the hole."**

"In the meantime, the hole is getting worse," said Theo. "It's getting bigger, and it's starting to warp other lines of code. It's like the whole game is mutating." He shrugged. "So my theory is that the Netherite Golem is somehow able to use that to its advantage. The game is changing, and the golem has some power over *how* it's changing. The golem is like a modder who's able to alter the code in real time . . . from the inside."

"Then let's hope the golem doesn't cheat when it's testing us," said Harper.

Po groaned. "Why does it have to be a test?" he asked.

"Hey, if it's a test . . . then we can study for it," said Morgan. He grinned. "Which means I've got some research to do."

The next day, during gym class, everyone was given free time to practice for their upcoming Field Day event. Harper and Theo ran the track, Po shot hoops, and Jodi worked on her throwing skills.

Morgan was stuck on the bleachers. But that suited him fine. **He had a lot of Minecraft reading to catch up on.**

The previous night, Morgan had loaded up his tablet with information about the Nether. **He was determined to prepare for the golem's test.** And he wasn't sure that he would be ready in time.

Morgan had only been to the Nether a handful of times since it had been updated with new biomes. Once, while playing alone at home, he'd gotten hopelessly lost. Another time, he'd been surprised by a blaze and knocked off a high perch, and he fell to his doom.

Of course, when you ran out of health in a normal game of Minecraft, you respawned. But that time, Morgan had lost all of his best equipment in the Nether. He hadn't gone back since.

And now he had no choice. **And he had**

no idea what would happen if he ran out of health in the strange version of Minecraft that the Evoker Spawn called home.

"Skipping gym? I don't blame you," said a voice. Morgan looked up and saw Mr. Mallory, the media specialist. "Most days, I would rather read than play sports."

Morgan lifted his injured foot. "It isn't up to me," he said. "I'm supposed to stay off my foot. I hurt it when I was climbing a tree over the weekend." He thought about that for a second. "Actually, the climbing part didn't hurt. It was falling *out* of the tree that caused the problem."

Mr. Mallory winced. "And that's exactly why

I prefer books." He peeked at the screen of Morgan's tablet. "Although *that* book might give me nightmares. Is that a pig-man?"

"A piglin," Morgan answered. "They're from Minecraft."

"I thought so," said Mr. Mallory. "You take that game very seriously, don't you?"

Morgan shrugged. **"I'm part of a team,"** he said. "My teammates count on me to know everything about the game."

"It sounds like they put a lot of pressure on you," said Mr. Mallory. "Unless you're putting the pressure on yourself?"

Morgan wasn't sure what the librarian meant by that. He was about to ask him, when Ms. Minerva's voice rang out: "There you are, Mr. Mallory! **Did you bring my books?"**

Mr. Mallory smiled as the teacher approached them. "That's why I'm here," he said.

"Disappointing!" said Doc as she hurried over from another direction. **"I had hoped you were here to deliver the hamster!"**

"I'm here for both reasons," said Mr. Mallory.

"I'm not choosing sides, remember?"

Now that Morgan saw the three adults in a row, he noticed something about their clothing. Ms. Minerva wore blue for her team, and Doc wore red for hers. Mr. Mallory was wearing *purple*. Morgan knew that purple was a combination of red and blue.

"You're still determined to stay neutral?" prodded Ms. Minerva.

"A pity!" said Doc. "Only supporters of Team Red will be allowed to use my high-tech massage chairs on Field Day."

Ms. Minerva clucked her tongue. "Those chairs will vibrate the fillings right out of your teeth."

Mr. Mallory didn't say anything. He put his backpack down on the bleachers, then zipped it open. He pulled out a small stack of books for Ms. Minerva. They were all about exercise and healthy eating.

"Knowledge shall win the day!" she said, and hurried off.

Next Mr. Mallory pulled out a small cage. Inside was Duchess Dimples, the library's hamster.

"Now both teams have a hamster," said Doc. "It's only fair!" She picked up the hamster's enclosure and scampered toward the school building.

Mr. Mallory shook his head. "See?" he said. "Sports do strange things to people. You're lucky you get to skip Field Day."

Morgan flushed red. **"I'm not skipping Field Day,"** he said. "I'll be better by then."

Mr. Mallory glanced at Morgan's injured foot. "I hope you're right," he said. "Good luck, Morgan, and feel better." With that, he headed back to the library, just as Harper and Theo approached.

Morgan quickly hid his tablet. He didn't want his friends to know that he was unprepared for the Nether. He especially didn't want Theo to realize it. **Theo's knowledge of Minecraft was almost equal to Morgan's,** and that sometimes made Morgan feel self-conscious. It felt a little bit like he and Theo were in competition, even though they were on the same team.

"Was that Duchess Dimples?" asked Harper. "What's she doing here?"

"Rooting for Team Red, apparently," answered

Morgan offhandedly.

"Speaking of Field Day," said Theo. "We have some concerns."

Morgan crossed his arms. "Like what?"

"We talked to Jodi," Theo said. "She said you'll be on crutches for at least another week."

"That isn't true!" Morgan insisted. "The doctor said it's impossible to know for sure. She said that everyone heals at their own speed!"

Harper raised her hand in a calming gesture. "We understand. And that's exactly why we're worried. We want you to heal, however long it takes. If you push yourself too hard, you could make your injury worse."

"We talked to Ms. Minerva," said Theo. "She said you can switch events. We just have to find a replacement."

"You want to *replace* me?" Morgan's jaw dropped. "No way! I'm telling you, I'll be fine. I feel a lot better already!" He turned to look directly at Harper. **"Don't give up on me, please."**

"Well, okay," Harper said hesitantly. "If you're sure."

"I'm sure," Morgan insisted. *"Really."*

Morgan made certain that his voice was steady and his eyes were calm. **But his leg hurt a little even as he said it.**

Chapter 5

IN A VAST VIDEO GAME FANTASY WORLD, THERE'S NOTHING QUITE LIKE NETHERITE, AMIRITE?

That afternoon, they returned to the Nether. The soul campfire was still burning. The Netherite Golem stood just where they had left it.

"We're ready," said Morgan. **"WE ACCEPT YOUR CHALLENGE."**

The golem's dark eyes twinkled. "Very good," said the mob. "Which one of you will be tested?"

Morgan tried to appear calm and confident as he stepped forward. It wasn't easy. The golem was much larger than him, with massive arms, broad shoulders, and dark eyes. Red vines twisted along its netherite body.

"Me. I'll go," said Morgan. "We took a vote."

The vote had been nearly unanimous, except Theo had voted for himself. And Po had voted for the class hamster, but Jodi had pointed out that the VR goggles wouldn't fit Baron Sweetcheeks.

The golem said, **"SO BE IT. LISTEN CAREFULLY, AND I WILL TELL YOU WHAT YOU MUST DO."**

Morgan nodded.

"North of here, there is a fortress. In the heart of that fortress is a chest. Within that chest is an item that I hold dear. Retrieve it, and I shall surrender to you."

"That's it?" Morgan said. **"I JUST HAVE TO FETCH YOUR PROPERTY?"**

"That's it," said the golem. Its square eyes gleamed with amusement. "But do not take the task lightly. The Nether is a dangerous place. Very dangerous. And you must each face it alone."

"**WHAT IF HE FAILS?**" asked Theo.

"Theo!" said Harper. "Have a little faith in Morgan."

"I'm not saying that I don't," said Theo. "But this is important information."

"If he fails, then another must try," answered the golem. "And then another. Until the item is retrieved . . . **OR UNTIL ALL FIVE HAVE FAILED.**"

"So we have five chances," said Theo.

"We don't need five chances," said Morgan. "You guys, I've got this."

"We know you do," said Po.

"We believe in you!" said Jodi.

"The chests are full of useful items," said the golem. "**TAKE WHATEVER YOU LIKE.**"

Morgan felt a thrill at those words. It never failed: opening a Minecraft chest to see what it held was even more exciting than unwrapping a birthday present.

And the golem's chests held quite a lot.

"Is this . . . netherite armor?" he asked. "And a sword! It would take forever to find enough netherite to make all of this!"

"WHAT'S NETHERITE?" asked Jodi.

"It's the strongest, most durable material in the whole game," Morgan answered, a huge smile on his avatar's face.

"I thought that was diamond," said his sister.

"It used to be," said Theo. "Netherite was added in an update."

Jodi threw up her blocky hands. "I can't keep up!" she said.

Morgan was still smiling. "All you need to know is that this stuff will make me unbeatable!" He began swapping out his old armor for the brand-new dark-gray upgrade.

"Hold on," said Theo. "Are you sure you should take the whole set?"

"Sure, I'm sure," said Morgan confidently. "Why wouldn't I?"

"Well . . . ," said Theo. **Morgan saw him trade a look with Harper.**

"I . . . think I see where Theo is coming from," said Harper. "Suppose you . . . don't succeed. Then one of *us* will have to go. And we'll have to do it without any netherite armor."

"What if you just took one piece?" suggested Theo. "Then there's some left for the rest of us."

"THAT'S A TERRIBLE SUGGESTION," said Morgan. "If I leave good gear behind, then

I'm making it less likely that I'll succeed. **IT'S SMARTER TO MAXIMIZE MY CHANCES."** He turned to Po and Jodi. "You two agree with me, right?"

Jodi nodded. "I want my brother to come back safe and sound. We can share the armor *after* you're back."

"Po?" prodded Morgan.

"Don't look at me," Po said. **"I VOTED FOR**

BARON SWEETCHEEKS!"

As far as Morgan was concerned, that settled it. If Theo or Harper was upset with him, he could apologize later, after he returned with the golem's trophy . . . or whatever it was.

"What am I looking for, by the way?" he asked the golem. "These chests are full of valuable loot. So what's the item that you're missing?"

"AN ITEM OF LITTLE VALUE . . . BUT GREAT WORTH," said the golem. "Bring it to me, Morgan Mercado." Its eyes glimmered in the light of the campfire. "Fail . . . and the consequences will be more severe than you can imagine."

Chapter 6

MORGAN MERCADO: ALONE IN THE NETHER! HE'S GOING TO NEED THAT ARMOR. AND A LOT OF LUCK!

Morgan's solo adventure in the Nether started off well.

He felt confident in his full set of netherite armor. And that's not all he'd taken from the golem's stash. He had a bow and arrows, cooked food, a shield to protect him from fireballs, and potions to provide a variety of benefits. In short, he felt prepared for whatever the Nether had to throw at him.

His first task was to travel through the warped forest. **It was full of Endermen,** but that was okay. Morgan had taken a pumpkin from the golem's chests. He wore it now, which allowed him

to pass among the Endermen untroubled.

If this whole challenge was a test, then so far, Morgan was on track for a perfect score.

The forest ended at a steep cliff wall. Morgan climbed it by carving out a staircase. He used a diamond pickaxe, which made it easy.

At the top of the cliff, Morgan gasped. He could see far off in the distance. The Nether was every bit as strange as he remembered. Great creatures floated in the air; they didn't see him yet. A ceiling blocked any view of sky, sun, or stars. **A vast ocean of lava stretched out before him,** leading to a soul sand shore. And past that, hazy in the distance, was a structure.

It was a bastion remnant. That had to be the "fortress" the golem had mentioned. **That's where he'd find its treasure.** He was sure of it.

He spared a brief glance backward. The warped forest spread out behind him. His friends were down there, depending on him. He couldn't see them through the trees, but he knew that they were there. He wouldn't let them down.

Morgan descended the cliff. **The sea of lava was below him.** It stretched out for a hundred blocks or more. He would have to find some way to cross it.

Unless . . . what if he went underneath?

It was a risky choice. But all his choices were risky, and digging a tunnel would at least keep him from drawing the attention of the flying mobs.

So he dug. He started by making a hole. When he was twenty blocks below ground level, he cut his way forward. Soon he was beneath the lava, traveling through an underground hallway of his own creation. **He placed torches as he went,** and he counted his steps.

Morgan knew that even a diamond pickaxe would wear down eventually. He took a quick look at the tool's durability bar, and he saw that it wouldn't last much longer. He had hoped to dig all the way to the fortress, but that would be impossible. So after counting one hundred steps, he started digging upward at an angle.

He struck lava almost immediately!

Clearly, one hundred steps had not been far enough. Morgan was still under the lava lake. And now the lava was surging forward, filling his tunnel. It reached for him like a hot, glowing hand, and as it touched him, he burned.

Morgan quickly placed a pair of netherrack blocks. The blocks were a dam, holding the lava back. But Morgan was still on fire!

He had thought something like this might happen. There were a lot of fire-related hazards in the Nether. **He pulled a Potion of Fire Resistance from his inventory,** and he drank it quickly. It kept him relatively safe while

he waited for the fire to go out.

In this version of Minecraft, Morgan could feel when he took damage. The lava and flames had been uncomfortable, and the potion's effect was cool and soothing on his digital skin.

"LET'S NOT DO THAT AGAIN," he said, and then he realized he was talking to himself. He missed his friends even more than he had thought he would.

Morgan cut his tunnel sideways, going around the spot where lava had filled it. He didn't try to dig upward again until he'd counted another hundred steps. This time, he drank a Potion of Fire Resistance first, but there was no lava. Only sky— or whatever passed for sky in the Nether.

Morgan hopped up aboveground. He knew he would need to identify what biome he was in quickly. **Every biome in the Nether carried new threats.**

He was immediately struck by arrows. He felt them, even through his powerful armor. He turned to run, but he was so *slow*. The sand at his feet was like wet cement.

He was in a soul sand valley.

Skeletons surrounded him, launching arrows in an endless attack.

Morgan drew his sword.

This was going to be a long day.

When he finally made it to the bastion remnant, Morgan was exhausted. He'd had to fight the whole way, and his armor and weapons were worn down nearly to breaking. He was out of potions, out of *food,* and his health was dangerously low.

Now he realized that he didn't have the one thing he needed most: **gold.**

The bastion remnant was crawling with piglins.

They were intimidating and strange. Morgan had encountered piglins in the past, of course. But not nearly as often as he'd seen the various mobs of the Overworld.

To Morgan, the most interesting fact about piglins was that they loved gold. **A hostile piglin would even become friendly for a time, if a player gave them gold.**

Wearing gold armor also worked. And there had been a gold helmet in the Netherite Golem's war chest. But Morgan had passed it up for a netherite helmet instead.

And his netherite armor had taken a lot of damage.

Morgan decided that a stealthy approach would be smart. He had a Potion of Invisibility . . . but he would have to remove his armor in order to become fully invisible. And that felt like too much of a risk, **even with his armor damaged.**

So Morgan took it slow. He hid behind a wall, then crouched as he worked his way to another wall. There were a lot of dark corners he could hide in. But that meant there were a lot of places

for piglins to hide, too. **Could he possibly avoid them all?**

The answer was no. One of the piglins spotted him. It made a horrible piglike sound.

Morgan leapt forward, swinging his netherite sword. He knocked back the piglin—too late. Its noises had already drawn the attention of its snouted siblings. With their swords and axes raised, they rushed to attack Morgan.

He swung his own sword in a wide arc. **He couldn't fight so many mobs.** But he hoped he could keep them back as he ran through the fortress.

Through a gap in the horde, he saw a lone treasure chest sitting out in the open. He was so close.

But also too far. One piglin attacked from behind, and as he turned to knock it away, two more got hits in.

They were swarming him now. There were too many. He felt like he was drowning.

Morgan buckled. He dropped to his knees.

"NO!" he said defiantly. "NO, I WON'T LOSE. I CAN'T!"

But Morgan did lose.

He lost consciousness and fell to the ground in utter defeat.

Chapter 7

BATTERED AND BEATEN. THE BITTER TASTE OF DEFEAT. WORSE THAN EATING YOUR VEGETABLES!

Jodi was startled. One second, she was with her friends in Minecraft, gazing into the eerie blue fire and waiting for her brother to return.

The next second, she was back in the computer lab at Stonesword Library.

Theo tore off his VR goggles. "We're back! It happened again."

Jodi quickly looked to make sure that Morgan was with them. He was, although he didn't look very happy about it. As he took off his goggles, he looked angry, and more than a little embarrassed.

"**I . . . I failed,**" he said, gripping his goggles tightly.

They all gasped. Even Jodi; she couldn't help herself.

Her brother was the master of Minecraft. He never failed!

"I came close," he said. "**Really close!** I could *see* the chest."

"I'm sure you did your best, Morgan," said Harper.

"I'll bet it was epic," said Po. "**Did you go down swinging?**"

"Yeah." Morgan smiled a little. "Yeah, I didn't give up without a fight."

"Well, there's some good news here," said Theo. "We've never been defeated in this version of Minecraft before. I was afraid there would be real-world consequences." He looked Morgan up and down. "But you seem to be okay. Do you feel all right?"

"I feel fine," said Morgan. He stretched. "I feel normal. But being defeated . . . it hurt. I could feel every blow, even through the netherite armor."

"And that's the bad news," said Theo. "You took all the best armor. And if this is working like Minecraft normally works, all your gear is now just lying there where you fell. It's not going to do us any good."

For a second, **Jodi thought that Morgan would say he was sorry.**

She thought that her brother might tell them what he'd seen, so that they could all learn from his defeat.

But Morgan obviously didn't like the way Theo was talking to him. It sounded like Theo was blaming Morgan for wasting the golem's loot.

So Morgan didn't apologize. He yelled instead. **"The netherite armor wouldn't help you!** If I couldn't win this challenge, none of you stand a chance. Armor isn't going to change that."

Jodi looked back at her brother, stunned. "Morgan!" she said. **"You don't mean that."**

"Good luck in the Nether, whoever goes next," said Morgan. "I'm not sticking around to watch you all fail one by one."

Then Morgan stormed out of Stonesword Library as fast as his crutches could take him.

For the next few hours, Jodi tried to make peace with her brother. But Morgan didn't make it easy for her.

He sulked on the ride home, gazing out the window the whole way.

He hid in his room before dinner, playing music loud enough to drown out her knocking.

She knew better than to bring up their **top-secret, high-tech, AI-infested, VR-infused Minecraft game** at dinner, where their parents would have all sorts of questions. Not

to mention the wild and dangerous adventures they sometimes faced.

But after dinner, she found him outside.

"What are you doing?" she asked him.

"Practicing," he said.

It looked a little reckless to Jodi. She watched as he hurried down the walkway, practically flinging himself across the stones. It was the fastest she'd ever seen someone move on crutches.

"Morgan, slow down!" she said. **"You're going to fall."**

"No, I'm not," he said through gritted teeth. But even as he said it, he stumbled badly. Luckily, he fell toward Jodi. She was able to catch him.

"Do I get to say I told you so?" she said.

Morgan scowled, and he pulled out of her grip. "You don't understand. I've got to get faster before Field Day. I don't want to slow Theo and Harper down. And I don't . . . **I don't want them to replace me."**

Jodi crossed her arms. "I don't know whether to try to make you feel better . . . or to tell you that you're being selfish."

Morgan sighed. He sat on the low garden wall. **"I vote for the first one,"** he said.

Jodi sat next to him. "Would it really be the end of the world if they did the relay race without you?"

"It's not just the relay race," said Morgan. "It's all this stuff with Minecraft and the Nether. I'm supposed to be the team expert! But Doc's VR goggles changed the game in weird ways, and then the Evoker King changed all sorts of things. And

today I couldn't even handle the Nether on my own. If I'd worn just a single piece of gold armor, I could have won."

"You can still win," said Jodi. "By helping *us* win. Harper is taking the challenge tomorrow. Tell her everything you know. Everything you saw! Were there giant piglins? Or Endermen with pitchforks?"

"It doesn't matter." Morgan shook his head. "Like Theo said, I wasted all the good items. I'm sorry, Jodi, but Harper doesn't stand a chance tomorrow." He got up and limped away. "And I won't be there to watch her be defeated. **She'll have to do it without me."**

Chapter 8

HARPER, HARPER, YOU CAN DO IT! RIGHT? BECAUSE, REALLY, THE WHOLE TEAM IS COUNTING ON YOU.

When the golem asked for the next volunteer, Harper stepped forward. She didn't hesitate. And though she felt a sliver of fear run through her, she didn't show it. **Whatever happened, her friends were there, cheering her on.**

Well . . . *most* of her friends were there. Morgan hadn't shown up at the library that day.

"Choose your tools," said the golem.

"IF THERE'S ANYTHING GOOD LEFT," Theo muttered, just loud enough for her to hear.

But Harper wasn't too worried about that. Morgan had taken a lot of useful items, but he hadn't bothered taking the useful *ingredients*.

Harper figured she would make her *own* items.

As luck would have it, the first chest she checked held an abundance of nether wart.

"This is perfect!" she said. **"MORGAN TOOK ALL THE POTIONS. BUT WITH THIS, I CAN BREW MY OWN."**

"What will you use potions for?" asked Jodi.

"There's a lot of lava in the Nether," said Harper. "Lava is very dangerous . . . **UNLESS YOU DRINK A POTION OF FIRE RESISTANCE.** Then it can't hurt you."

Po's mouth dropped open. "So you're planning

to *swim* in lava? Harper, you're my hero!"

Harper grinned. "Pretty cool, right? Just don't try this at Field Day, kids."

Harper traveled through the warped forest, over the cliff, and down to the shore of the great lava lake. It stretched out nearly as far as she could see. She would have to be quick.

She drank down her freshly brewed, orange-hued potion in a single gulp. Then she prepared to dive—but she hesitated. She had faith in her potion; she was sure she'd done it right. Still, the thought of entering the lava made her nervous.

But there was no turning back now. **She dove headfirst into the lava.** She didn't feel a thing!w

Harper began swimming. She knew she had only a few minutes before the potion would wear off, so she had to move quickly..

When she had made it halfway across the lake,

she realized she would not make it the rest of the way in time. But that was okay. **Harper had planned for this.**

She set some stone blocks in front of her, creating a small, two-by-two stone island in the middle of the lake. She hopped onto the island and set down her brewing stand. Then she made another potion, and she drank it immediately.

She decided to leave the brewing stand where it was. It would be useful on the way back. She even left some key ingredients behind, so that she'd be able to brew again in a hurry.

As Harper swam, **a shadow passed over**

her. It startled her. There were no clouds in the Nether. What could it be?

She looked up, and a great, fearsome ghast was just above her. Its tentacles hung low, and it made a strange mewing sound.

Harper dove beneath the surface. Had the ghast seen her? She waited for several seconds. Soon, she could wait no longer. **She had to come up for a breath!**

Harper swam up. To her relief, the ghast had drifted away.

But then Harper realized she had lost precious seconds. How long had she been beneath the lava?

She hesitated with indecision. Should she hurry toward the far shore? Should she turn around and return to her island of stone and brew another potion?

The hesitation cost her. **Her time was up.**

Harper could suddenly feel the heat of the lava. It gripped her like a fiery fist. She could see the flames all along her arms!

Harper yelled for help, **but no one was close enough to hear her.**

"Harper! Are you okay?"

Harper blinked. She realized she was safe in the library. Theo and the others looked at her with concern. **Had she been yelling in real life?**

Mr. Mallory came hurrying around the corner. "What's going on?" he asked.

"I'm sorry, Mr. Mallory," she said. "I was playing a video game, and my avatar was trapped in lava. It . . . it seemed so real."

Theo frowned as he realized what

this meant. Harper had failed the golem's challenge.

But Mr. Mallory smiled. "Thank goodness. I thought something was really wrong."

"Everything's fine, honest," Harper said. She was embarrassed by all the attention. **Her cheeks grew hot.**

It felt a little bit like she was still in that unforgiving lake of lava.

Chapter 9

THEO, THEO, HE'S OUR MAN! IF HE CAN'T DO IT, NO ONE CAN! BUT NO PRESSURE. NOPE, NONE AT ALL.

Theo was determined to succeed where his friends had failed. He didn't even wait for the golem to ask. He strode right up to the mob and announced: "I'm next."

"CHOOSE YOUR TOOLS," said the golem. Theo thought there was a hint of amusement in the golem's tone.

Theo rummaged through the chests in search of anything that might be useful. There wasn't much left. But to his surprise, there was a particularly useful—**and especially rare**—item in the last chest he checked.

"ELYTRA!" he said, his voice full of awe. He

turned to his friends, smiling.
"I don't need to swim across the lava.
Not when I have wings!"

"Wow!" said Jodi. **"DO THOSE THINGS
LET YOU FLY?"**

"It's more like gliding than flying," Theo said.
He tried on the elytra, which were similar to some
sort of geometric beetle wings that attached to his
shoulders. "I'll have to start from up high so I can
drift across the lava."

Minutes later, as Theo looked out upon the great
orange sea, he realized that the cliff separating the
warped forest from the lava lake was not nearly
high enough.

So Theo built. Jumping in place, he dropped
blocks of dirt beneath his feet. Soon, he stood atop
a narrow column of dirt. He could see the bastion
remnant!

But he still wouldn't be able to glide that far.
He would have to aim for the soul sand valley on
the other side of the lava. It was the closest point.

Theo wished he had fingers to cross. Instead, he pressed his blocky fists together. "I got this," he said.

And then he jumped into the air.

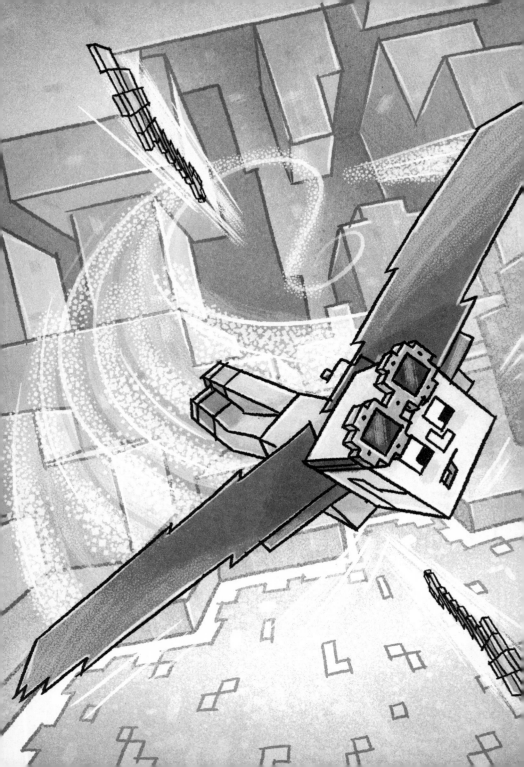

The experience was thrilling. Theo had always enjoyed flying in Minecraft, back when he had played in Creative mode. But this was a different experience. Doc's VR technology made him feel as if he were really, truly gliding through the air!

Theo's excitement slowly faded, and fear grew in its place. He was losing height every second, getting closer and closer to the lava below—even starting to feel the heat. He was pretty sure he would make it to the other side. But it was going to be close.

And then an arrow whizzed by him.

Theo veered wildly in the air. Where did that come from?

He found the answer below and ahead of him. On the shore of the soul sand valley, a cluster of skeletons had gathered. **Each one held a bow, and each one was looking his way.**

Up in the air, there was nowhere to hide, and no way to fight back. Theo would just have to hope he could reach land before he took too many hits.

As more arrows flew in his direction, Theo went

on the defensive. **He rolled, he banked, he dove.** He did anything and everything he could to avoid the projectiles.

And he did a great job. He didn't get hit even once!

Unfortunately, Theo realized too late that there was a problem. All of his fancy moves had cost him precious time in the air. He wasn't much closer to land.

But he was much, much closer to the lava. Too close!

Theo splashed down into the glowing orange liquid. His avatar caught fire, wings and all.

Back in the computer lab, Theo angrily removed his goggles.

"**That wasn't fair!**" he said. "I was a sitting duck for those skeletons."

"It's okay, Theo," said Harper. "At least you're safe."

"Sure," said Theo. "And I learned an important lesson, too. **Flying is for the birds!**"

Chapter 10

WE MEANT PO. IF HE CAN'T DO IT, NO ONE CAN! AND WE HOPE HE CAN DO IT, BECAUSE WE ARE REALLY STARTING TO RUN OUT OF OPTIONS!

Po had never thought of himself as much of a builder.

Some Minecraft players liked to mine. Others liked to craft. **Po enjoyed the exploration and adventure aspect of the game the most.** He liked imagining himself as a heroic character, finding new biomes, and striking down gruesome undead enemies.

But as he prepped by the golem's fire with his friends, he realized something. After accepting the golem's challenge and looking through the mostly empty chests, he realized: he would have to build . . . something.

"IT'S MOSTLY DIRT AND STONE AND NETHERRACK LEFT," he said. "Although there is another pair of elytra, and a gold helmet."

Theo shook his head. "The elytra won't do you any good. Maybe if we had a rocket, but we don't. And there's no gunpowder to make one."

"AND YOUR DIAMOND HELMET IS WAY BETTER THAN A GOLD ONE," said Harper.

"It looks nicer, too," Jodi added.

"I know!" said Po. "It sparkles."

"Focus, Po!" said Theo. "Do you have a plan for crossing the lava?"

"I've got a lot of building material," said Po. "SO IT LOOKS LIKE I'LL BE BUILDING A BRIDGE."

Po's inventory was almost entirely full of blocks. He was glad they didn't weigh anything. He wouldn't want to carry around stacks of stone cubes in real life.

Building a bridge wasn't the most exciting

experience. He was a little jealous of his friends. Theo had flown through the air! Harper had done the butterfly stroke in hot lava!

But as Po peered over the side of his makeshift bridge and into the lava below, he shuddered. He was actually quite happy to be on solid ground and away from the molten red-hot rock he could feel even at this distance.

And then, mere minutes after he had started, **Po realized he was running out of blocks.**

"Huh," said Po. He stood at the unfinished edge of his bridge. The far shore was still quite far.

He saw the problem now. **He'd been**

making his bridge too wide. He didn't exactly want to walk a balance beam across the lava. But a narrower bridge would reach farther.

Po quickly dismantled the structure, removing the blocks and starting again. It just might work if his building materials held out. **He wished his block hands had fingers so he could cross them for good luck.**

As Po turned around to retrieve more blocks from behind him, he looked back at his starting point. He could see the warped forest, and there was movement between the trees. **It was a tall figure with glowing eyes.** Was the golem watching him? The figure looked at Po, and Po looked right back.

And then Po realized his mistake. That wasn't the Netherite Golem. That was an Enderman!

Po looked away quickly. He knew Endermen didn't like to be looked at. Had he turned away in time?

A low moan sounded from nearby. Po looked up and saw that he was no longer alone on his partial

bridge. The Enderman had teleported right next to him!

Po shrieked. Unarmed, he slapped at the Enderman, hoping it would teleport away.

But the Enderman slapped right back. Po leapt backward to avoid the blow—right over the edge of his structure . . .

And into the waiting lava below.

"Oh, man," said Po. He had opened his eyes to find himself back at Stonesword Library. **"That's it. From now on, I'm wearing a pumpkin everywhere I go."**

"A pumpkin?" said Jodi.

"Let me guess," said Harper. "You must have run into an Enderman problem."

"You're not supposed to look directly at them," said Theo.

"I know, Theo!" said Po. "I didn't do it on purpose." He shook his head. **"They say curiosity killed the cat.** But they *should* say that curiosity got Po knocked off the edge of his bridge and into the lava."

"It's kind of a mouthful," said Jodi.

"It's true, though," said Po. **"And it means we've only got one more chance to win."**

Chapter 11

A TWIST OF FATE! A TWIST OF ANKLE! THIS CHAPTER'S GOT MORE TWISTS THAN THE LATEST DANCE CRAZE.

Morgan felt a little guilty, hearing how his friends had fared without him.

They were gathered on the Woodsword playground, and Po was telling the story of his half-built bridge. "I'm telling you, I've got a fear of heights after that experience," he said. **"And also a fear of teleporting monsters, and lava, and sad clowns wearing little hats."**

"Wait, there were clowns there, too?" asked Jodi in surprise.

"No," said Po. "I've just always been creeped out by them. The sad ones, especially." He shuddered.

Harper patted Po's arm. "I really thought that

plan would work," she said. **"The Nether is too dangerous."**

"That means it's up to you, Jodi," said Theo. "You're our last hope."

Jodi chuckled nervously. "Wow! No pressure, though, right?"

Theo frowned. "It's quite a lot of pressure, actually."

Jodi rolled her eyes and said, "Does Woodsword have any classes on understanding sarcasm? Because you might learn a thing or two." Then she groaned and dropped her head into her hands.

Morgan cleared his throat. "I have an idea," he said.

Po shook his head. "If your idea is to tell the golem all about Baron Sweetcheeks, you're too

late! I chatted the golem's ear off the whole time Theo was running the challenge."

"It's true," Harper confirmed. "You know, the golem doesn't close its eyes, but I could almost swear it dozed off once or twice."

"I'm pretty sure it was just drinking it all in," Po replied with a huff.

Theo frowned. "Or maybe Morgan's idea is to go back in time and help us before we all suffered a series of defeats?"

"Not helpful, Theo," Harper said in a singsong voice.

"I guess he *does* understand sarcasm after all," Jodi said. Then, without lifting her face from her hands, she asked her brother, "What's your idea, Morgan?"

"Let me try again, said Morgan. **"Jodi can give me her spot, and I'll use what I learned last time to succeed."**

Jodi lifted her head. *"That's not fair!"*

"It might be smart, though," Theo said. "I mean, he has a point."

"Were you even excited for your turn, Jodi?" Po

asked. "It seemed like you were worried."

"That's not the point," Jodi said.

"I'm not sure the golem will allow it," Harper said. "It told us we had five chances. But it strongly implied we'd only get one chance each."

"The golem's a computer program," said Theo. "If our argument is logical, we can convince it."

"First you've got to convince me!" said Jodi.

Morgan excused himself, leaving his friends to debate his proposal.

Field Day was only a day away. And he had to fit in one last practice.

Morgan was getting faster. He was sure of it. His underarms were rubbed raw, and his good foot was getting a blister, but that was the price he had to pay for speed.

He set a stopwatch. He wanted to time how long it took him to make one circuit around the school track.

Everyone else was at lunch. That's why Morgan chose to practice now. He wanted some privacy.

But there was one problem with that.

It meant that when he fell . . . nobody was there to catch him.

Chapter 12

NURSE YOUR WOUNDS, NOT YOUR GRUDGES! WOUNDS HEAL, BUT GRUDGES JUST GET WORSE.

Morgan spent a good part of the afternoon in the nurse's office. He had twisted his ankle. The pain had been excruciating—even worse than the first injury—but there was good news.

"**Nothing's broken,**" said Doc. "And you didn't do any permanent damage. But you have *got* to rest, Morgan. You'll never heal if you keep landing on it funny."

Morgan nodded. "I've learned my lesson. **Pain is a great teacher.**"

"As long as *this* great teacher isn't a pain!" said Doc. She chortled at her own joke, but Morgan could only moan.

"**It sounds like he's in pain!**" cried Jodi as she pushed her way into the cramped office. Harper, Theo, and Po were right behind her.

"I'm afraid we can't save his sense of humor," said Doc. "But his foot will be fine . . . in a couple of weeks."

"Doc?" said Harper. "**I didn't know you were our school nurse.**"

"Just filling in while Glenda is on vacation," Doc said. "As long as nobody needs a kidney transplant, I can handle it." She seemed to sense

some tension between Morgan and his visitors. "I'll let you all talk, but I'll be right outside if you need me."

Po waited until Doc had left, and then he turned to Morgan. "Dude, we were so worried!" he said. "When you weren't in class, we didn't know what happened."

"We even called Ash," said Harper. She held up her phone. **Morgan could see the face of their long-distance friend, Ash, on the screen.**

"Hi, Morgan," said Ash. "I'm glad to see you're

okay. Jodi thought you'd run away to join the circus."

"Or to play Minecraft without us," said Theo. "We actually checked the library first."

Morgan shook his head. "I guess I haven't been much of a team player lately, have I? But I wouldn't have gone behind your backs like that."

"Can you tell us why you've been so upset?" Ash asked.

"Well . . ." Morgan felt his cheeks get hot. "I

guess it's because I like being a part of this team so much. And I worry sometimes that you don't need me. Or even that I'm holding you back."

"Holding us back?" said Po. "That's the opposite of what you do."

"But I'm supposed to be the Minecraft expert," said Morgan. "And I've been so busy that I haven't been able to keep up like I used to. I wasn't prepared to face the Nether alone, and sometimes Theo knows more than I do."

"Two heads are a lot better than one," said Theo. "When it comes to knowledge, everybody contributes."

"Theo's right," said Harper. "I mean, I've always been better at remembering crafting formulas."

Jodi chuckled. "That's true! Just like I'm good at taming cute animal mobs."

"And if we have to replace you on a relay race, that *wouldn't* mean we're replacing you as a friend, you know," Harper continued. "We don't even care that much about winning the race. We just didn't want you to get hurt again."

"Mission *not* accomplished," Po said, pointing at Morgan's freshly rebraced foot.

"I guess I took it too personally," said Morgan. "I was looking forward to being on a team with you two for Field Day. I didn't want to miss out. **But I have to face facts. And that means staying off my foot for a while.**" He looked from Harper to Theo. "What will you do now?"

"We'll think of something," said Theo. "In the relay race *and* in Minecraft."

"I'm sorry I tried to take your spot,

Jodi," said Morgan.

She sighed. "That's okay. Honestly, I'm worried. I wish we could all do the golem's challenge together."

"Maybe, in a way . . . you can," Ash said through the phone.

Morgan grinned. "It sounds like you have an idea."

Ash nodded. "The golem is making you work as individuals. But maybe you can treat its game less like a competition." She smiled. "And more like a relay race."

Chapter 13

JODI AND THE PIGLINS. SOUNDS LIKE A BAND! AND SPEAKING OF MUSIC, ARE YOU READY TO NETHERRACK AND ROLL?!

The golem didn't ask for a volunteer. It looked at the five avatars gathered around the campfire and said, "Jodi. Choose your items."

Jodi was ready. She had given it a lot of thought and consulted her friends. The elytra would help, and so would an empty flask and the gleaming golden helmet.

But the real tool Jodi had was knowledge. Her friends had told her everything she would need to know **in order to survive the Nether and return with the golem's prize.**

At least, she hoped so.

She kept her head down as she navigated the

warped forest. There were Endermen all around her, and her gold helmet wouldn't offer much protection from them. But as long as she minded her own business, they would leave her alone.

She climbed the cliff and saw Po's bridge right away. It extended out over the sea of lava like an Olympic diving platform. She saw the hole to Morgan's tunnel, too. But she knew the tunnel would lead her right into the heart of a soul sand valley—and lots of skeletons to get past. The bridge was the safer choice. **She walked to its very edge.** She could see the soul sand valley in the distance.

Jodi donned her elytra. With a running start, she leapt off the edge of Po's platform.

It was exhilarating to fly again after so long. **Jodi used to fly all the time in Creative mode.** She couldn't help laughing as the Nether stretched out before her.

But she knew better than to glide all the way to the soul sand. The skeletons there would only shoot her out of the sky, as they did to Theo.

Instead, she aimed for a small stone island in the middle of the lava. It was easy to spot from the air, and she reached it with no problems.

Harper had left the brewing stand behind, **with just enough material for one more Potion of Fire Resistance.** Jodi had never made one before, but she remembered Harper's instructions. Within seconds, her empty flask was filled with a liquid that looked a little like orange soda.

Jodi drank the potion. Then she looked at the lava with a bit of dread. But Harper had told her there was nothing to worry about . . . as long as she was quick. **So, without wasting another second, she dove into the lava.** She stayed beneath the surface, where she would be safe from any ghasts flying overhead.

Her brother had had to fight his way through the soul sand valley, where the sand was hazardous and the monsters were numerous. Jodi went around the other way so that she could travel through a crimson forest instead. There were dangers here, but they were easier to avoid. She took it slow, darting from tree to tree. Soon, she had arrived at the bastion remnant.

The structure was crawling with piglins. They saw her approach, and she held her breath. **There was no way she could fight them all!**

But the piglins didn't attack. They didn't seem the least bit bothered by her. A baby piglin even walked right up to her. It was cute!

Morgan's advice had worked. **As long as she wore a gold helmet,** she would be safe

among the piglins.

Still, she didn't want them to see her stealing from them. She waited until she was alone before she approached the treasure chest at the center of the bastion. Would she find glittering jewels, precious materials, or framed works of art?

Instead, the chest held a random assortment of items. **There was a**

black disc, a saddle, and a fishing rod with a strange-looking mushroom on its hook.

There was also an illustration. It showed Jodi what to do with the fishing rod and saddle.

"NO. WAY," she said, smiling excitedly in the moment.

She still had to get back to the others, which meant crossing the lava once more.

But this time, she would be traveling in style.

Jodi's friends were waiting for her on the far shore. She could see the looks of surprise and delight on their faces as they realized she was riding a strider.

The strider was a strange creature,

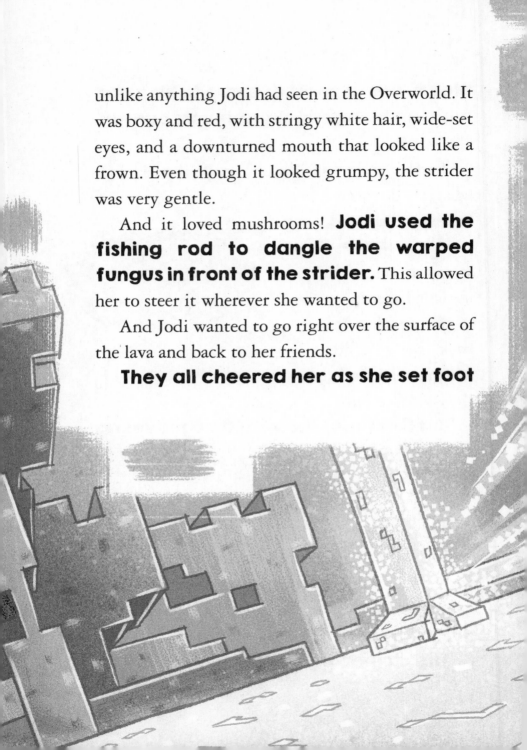

unlike anything Jodi had seen in the Overworld. It was boxy and red, with stringy white hair, wide-set eyes, and a downturned mouth that looked like a frown. Even though it looked grumpy, the strider was very gentle.

And it loved mushrooms! **Jodi used the fishing rod to dangle the warped fungus in front of the strider.** This allowed her to steer it wherever she wanted to go.

And Jodi wanted to go right over the surface of the lava and back to her friends.

They all cheered her as she set foot

safely on shore. She cheered them right back. After all, thanks to Ash's idea, this had been a team effort. Jodi was only able to win because her friends had paved the way for her. Even better, they had shared what they had learned, and Jodi was able to avoid making the same mistakes.

She patted the strider and placed the weird fungus on the ground in front of it. "Thanks for the lift, Stri-Guy," she said.

"**YOU HAVE THE ITEM?**" asked the golem.

"I think so," said Jodi, and she held out the black disc. "But I thought it would be a treasure. What makes this thing so valuable?"

"The item itself is not precious," said the golem. "**BUT THE JOY IT BRINGS IS PRICELESS.**"

With that, the golem directed Jodi to place the disc into a slotted brown box. It was a jukebox, and once the disc was in place, music poured forth.

"Is that . . . ?" asked Morgan.

"'Pigstep'!" said Theo.

"Pig does what now?" asked Po.

Harper laughed and said, "**'PIGSTEP.' IT'S THE NAME OF THE SONG.**"

"It's catchy!" said Jodi, and she began dancing to the beat. The other kids joined in . . . and to Jodi's surprise, so did the golem.

The mob had been so stony and unemotional. But at the sound of the music, **the golem seemed to truly come alive.** It swayed its hips. It waved its arms. And its eyes glinted with delight.

This was the Evoker King's joy, Jodi knew. The golem was the part of their friend that delighted in all the wonders of Minecraft.

As they danced, the golem began to glow. **Then its body transformed into a swirling mass of butterflies.** The butterflies fluttered and swayed in their own dance before rushing past Jodi on their way back toward the portal.

They left behind a piece of the Evoker King. Morgan called it the torso.

Jodi smiled, knowing it was really the Evoker King's heart.

Chapter 14

FIELD DAY! IN WHICH BARON SWEETCHEEKS SHOWS HIS TRUE COLORS AND EVERYONE HAS A GREAT TIME!

Field Day had come at last to Woodsword Middle School. Morgan wouldn't have missed it for the world—even though he was still on crutches, and on strict orders to stay off his foot.

"Good to see you, Team Blue!" Ms. Minerva said when Morgan entered the school. He was wearing his team color and a bib with his participant number: 43. She checked him off a list.

"Wait a minute," said the teacher. She looked at his crutches. **"Number forty-three, I have you down for the relay race. That can't be right."**

"**Sure it is,**" said Morgan. "I missed the deadline to change my event. So participant number forty-three will definitely do the relay race."

Po came forward on his wheelchair to greet Morgan with a high five. (It made Morgan wobble, but he didn't fall.) Po was also wearing blue, and his bib number was 13. **He was already set to deck his wheelchair out like an ancient Greek chariot!**

"You ready to make the trade?" Po asked him.

Morgan grinned. "Let's do it."

As Ms. Minerva watched, the boys removed their numbered bibs—and traded them. Morgan affixed **number 13** to his shirt, while Po took **number 43** for his own.

Ms. Minerva smiled. "A brilliant display of problem-solving," she said. "Participants forty-three and thirteen, enjoy your events. **And do Team Blue proud out there!**"

Later that morning, wearing Morgan's bib, Po

took his place on the track. Theo and Harper were there, too, along with the relay runners for the red, gold, and green teams.

Morgan and Jodi watched from the bleachers, along with a couple of very special guests—**Baron Sweetcheeks and Duchess Dimples!**

"Let's go, Team Blue! Let's go, Red!" cried Jodi. "Duchess Dimples is rooting for both of you!"

Theo called from the sidelines, "Actually, hamsters are almost entirely color-blind!"

Jodi called back, "She is no longer rooting for you! She's just squeaking enthusiastically in your general direction!"

A bell sounded, signaling the start of the race. Harper took an early lead, sprinting ahead of her competition. But she used too much energy too soon, and the other teams caught up just as she handed the baton to Theo.

Theo stumbled a little as he started, and the other racers pulled ahead. But as Morgan watched, Theo churned his arms and legs. He kept his eyes ahead of him, and he quickly reached Po sooner than they thought he could.

Po shot forward in his wheelchair, as fast as Morgan had ever seen him move. Po's time on the basketball court had obviously made him quite adept at bursts of speed.

Po started in last place. He overtook Team Gold, and then Team Green . . . but Team Red finished just ahead of him.

"Second place!" said Jodi. **"That's great!"**

"It is," said Morgan, clapping furiously ... while being careful not to knock Baron Sweetcheeks and Duchess Dimples over.

The hamster seemed unimpressed with the race. **The whole time, he only had eyes for the Duchess.**

Jodi's event was discus throwing. **She got first place in the competition despite a wild first throw that almost gave Ms. Minerva a surprise haircut.**

And then it was Morgan's turn. At first, he felt pressure to do as well as his sister had. Winning first place would feel really good!

But then he remembered: he was supposed to be having *fun,* not stressing himself out. At Ms. Minerva's suggestion, **he even tried meditating.** It calmed him down a little. He especially liked focusing on his breathing.

The free-throw basketball event would not have been Morgan's first choice. He wasn't a natural at

shooting hoops. But because Woodsword had a title-winning wheelchair basketball team, no one had any problem with Morgan making his shots from a seated position. That way, he was able to stay off his feet, and he didn't have to worry about losing his balance.

He only made two baskets, though. That left him in last place.

It didn't matter. **He laughed when he missed a basket, and he hooted with joy when he made one.**

And his friends were there on the sidelines, cheering him on the whole time.

Chapter 15

EVERYBODY LOVES A HAPPY ENDING! WHICH MEANS YOU'RE PROBABLY GOING TO REALLY HATE THIS PART.

A few days passed before Morgan and his friends were able to return to Minecraft. It was their first time donning their goggles since they had won the golem's game.

There was just one more piece of the Evoker King to retrieve. Just one!

They spawned at the blue soul fire camp, where they checked the golem's chests for good measure. The chests were empty. They had already gone through every bit of the golem's loot.

"WE'RE RUNNING REALLY LOW ON . . . EVERYTHING," said Harper.

"That's all right," said Theo. "We'll be able to

resupply in the Overworld."

"I am so ready to get out of this place," said Po.

"I'll sort of miss the piglins, to be honest," said Jodi.

Morgan shuddered thinking about the piglike mobs. "Not me. **COME ON, LET'S GO.**"

At the portal, Morgan wondered briefly what they'd see on the other side. It had been more than a week since they'd been in the Overworld. The last time they'd seen it, **the Fault had swallowed the entire sky.** He hoped it hadn't gotten any worse.

That hope was in vain.

Morgan's virtual jaw dropped open as he stepped out into the Overworld. It was unrecognizable. The Fault was everywhere. **A pixelated, lightning-lanced abyss of darkness stretched out above, before, and below them.** The landscape was still there—he had land beneath his feet—but it was cracked and segmented. It looked more like the floating islands of the End than the Overworld he knew and loved.

His friends came through the portal behind

him. One by one, they all gasped.

"What happened here?" asked Jodi.

"We're too late," Morgan told her. **"THE FAULT . . . IT'S SWALLOWED THE WHOLE OVERWORLD!"**

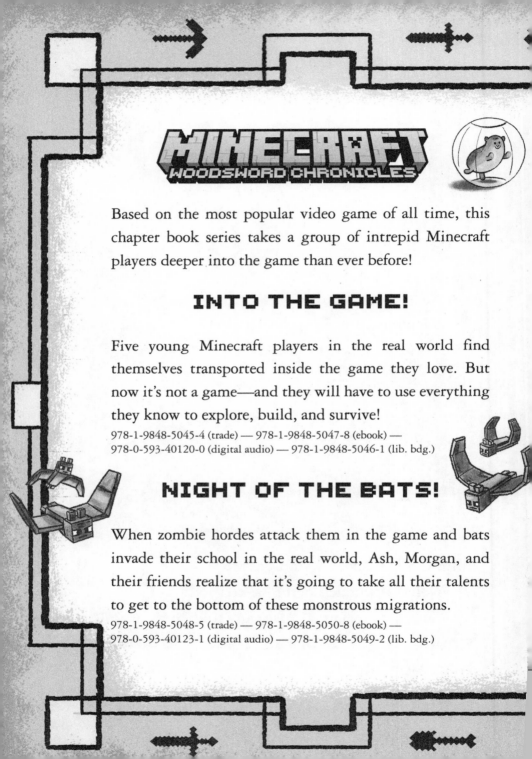

MINECRAFT
WOODSWORD CHRONICLES

Based on the most popular video game of all time, this chapter book series takes a group of intrepid Minecraft players deeper into the game than ever before!

INTO THE GAME!

Five young Minecraft players in the real world find themselves transported inside the game they love. But now it's not a game—and they will have to use everything they know to explore, build, and survive!

978-1-9848-5045-4 (trade) — 978-1-9848-5047-8 (ebook) — 978-0-593-40120-0 (digital audio) — 978-1-9848-5046-1 (lib. bdg.)

NIGHT OF THE BATS!

When zombie hordes attack them in the game and bats invade their school in the real world, Ash, Morgan, and their friends realize that it's going to take all their talents to get to the bottom of these monstrous migrations.

978-1-9848-5048-5 (trade) — 978-1-9848-5050-8 (ebook) — 978-0-593-40123-1 (digital audio) — 978-1-9848-5049-2 (lib. bdg.)

DEEP DIVE!

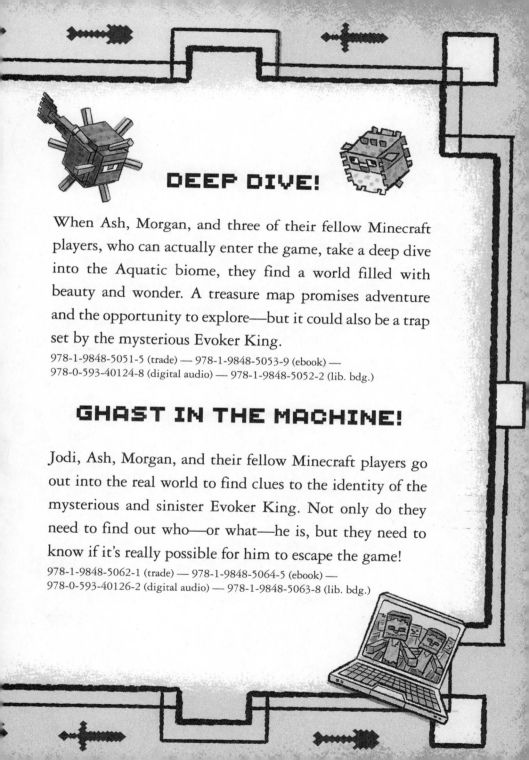

When Ash, Morgan, and three of their fellow Minecraft players, who can actually enter the game, take a deep dive into the Aquatic biome, they find a world filled with beauty and wonder. A treasure map promises adventure and the opportunity to explore—but it could also be a trap set by the mysterious Evoker King.

978-1-9848-5051-5 (trade) — 978-1-9848-5053-9 (ebook) — 978-0-593-40124-8 (digital audio) — 978-1-9848-5052-2 (lib. bdg.)

GHAST IN THE MACHINE!

Jodi, Ash, Morgan, and their fellow Minecraft players go out into the real world to find clues to the identity of the mysterious and sinister Evoker King. Not only do they need to find out who—or what—he is, but they need to know if it's really possible for him to escape the game!

978-1-9848-5062-1 (trade) — 978-1-9848-5064-5 (ebook) — 978-0-593-40126-2 (digital audio) — 978-1-9848-5063-8 (lib. bdg.)

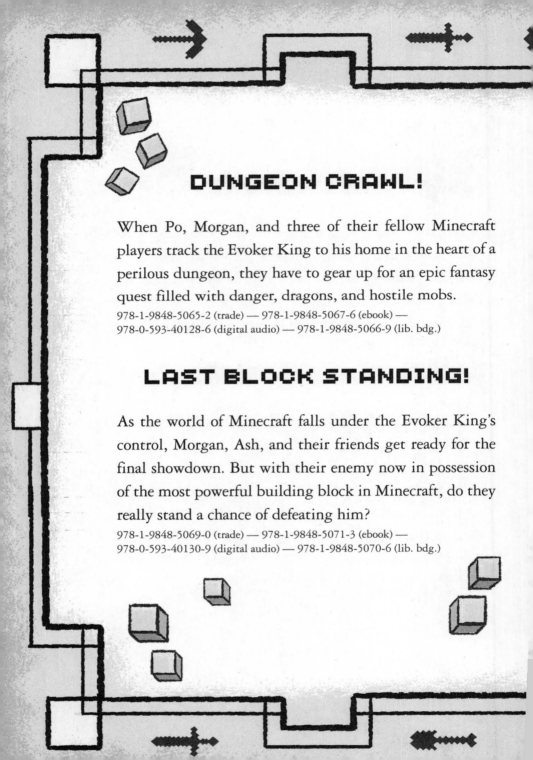

DUNGEON CRAWL!

When Po, Morgan, and three of their fellow Minecraft players track the Evoker King to his home in the heart of a perilous dungeon, they have to gear up for an epic fantasy quest filled with danger, dragons, and hostile mobs.

978-1-9848-5065-2 (trade) — 978-1-9848-5067-6 (ebook) — 978-0-593-40128-6 (digital audio) — 978-1-9848-5066-9 (lib. bdg.)

LAST BLOCK STANDING!

As the world of Minecraft falls under the Evoker King's control, Morgan, Ash, and their friends get ready for the final showdown. But with their enemy now in possession of the most powerful building block in Minecraft, do they really stand a chance of defeating him?

978-1-9848-5069-0 (trade) — 978-1-9848-5071-3 (ebook) — 978-0-593-40130-9 (digital audio) — 978-1-9848-5070-6 (lib. bdg.)

THE ADVENTURES CONTINUE IN

MINECRAFT STONESWORD SAGA

CRACK IN THE CODE!

Someone—or something—has turned the Evoker King to stone. And now a new player, Theo, has joined the team on their quest to return their former enemy to normal. Theo has modding skills that could come in handy, but does he have what it takes to be part of the team, or will his meddling put a crack in the game code that none of them will survive?

978-0-593-37298-2 (trade) — 978-0-593-37300-2 (ebook) — 978-0-593-40132-3 (digital audio) — 978-0-593-37299-9 (lib. bdg.)

MOBS RULE!

Po, Harper, and their friends must travel deep underground and into a web of danger. But that's the easy part, because in the real world, Po decides to run for class president, and before he knows it, the ground feels like it's opening under his feet!

978-1-9848-5075-1 (trade) — 978-1-9848-5077-5 (ebook) — 978-0-593-50552-6 (digital audio) — 978-1-9848-5076-8 (lib. bdg.)

NEW PETS ON THE BLOCK!

When the third piece of the Evoker King takes the form of a Minecraft witch and sends Jodi, Morgan, and their friends on a quest to bring back an extremely rare animal mob, Jodi is determined to make sure that the mob stays safe no matter what!

978-1-9848-5094-2 (trade) — 978-1-9848-5096-6 (ebook) — 978-0-593-55978-9 (digital audio) — 978-1-9848-5095-9 (lib. bdg.)

TOO BEE, OR NOT TO BEE!

The bees around the school and the Stonesword Library are disappearing—and a splinter of the Evoker King has taken on the form of a bee colony with a hive mind! Could there be a connection? And to make matters worse, the rip in the Minecraft sky is growing bigger and darker.

978-0-593-56288-8 (trade) — 978-0-593-56290-1 (ebook) — 978-0-593-66817-7 (digital audio) — 978-0-593-56289-5 (lib. bdg.)

GET READY FOR THE EPIC CONCLUSION TO THE STONESWORD SAGA IN BOOK 6—COMING SOON!

MINECRAFT is a game about placing blocks and going on adventures. Build, play, and explore across infinitely generated worlds of mountains, caverns, oceans, jungles, and deserts. Defeat hordes of zombies, bake the cake of your dreams, venture to new dimensions, or build a skyscraper. What you do in Minecraft is up to you.

Nick Eliopulos is a writer who lives in Brooklyn (as many writers do). He likes to spend half his free time reading and the other half gaming. He cowrote the Adventurers Guild series with his best friend and works as a narrative designer for a small video game studio. After all these years, endermen still give him the creeps.